SOMETHING'
SA

Sarah led Midnight over to the Takamuras' stables, past the Pony Tails.

Suddenly Sam bucked. A surprised Corey flew off his back and landed on the ground with a thud.

"We'll get him!" Jasmine cried. She and May sprang into action, chasing after Sam on their ponies.

Corey stood up. Luckily she wasn't hurt. The really scary part was how suddenly Sam had acted up – his bad behaviour had come as a complete surprise.

A few minutes later May led Sam back and handed his reins to Corey.

"You're a naughty pony," Corey started to scold Sam. Then she noticed the wild look in Sam's eyes.

Sam wasn't being naughty – he was scared!

Don't miss any of the titles in the
PONY TAILS series:

BONNIE BRYANT

PONY TAILS™

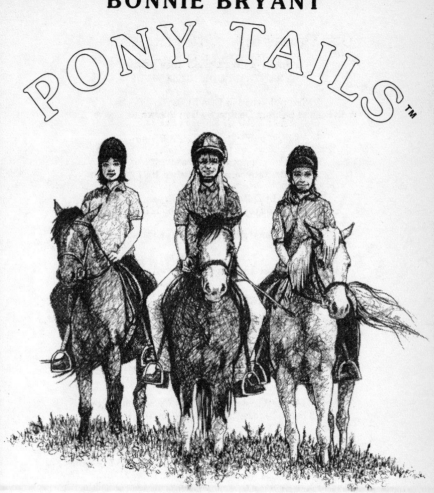

Corey and the Spooky Pony

BANTAM BOOKS
TORONTO · NEW YORK · LONDON · SYDNEY · AUCKLAND

COREY AND THE SPOOKY PONY
A BANTAM BOOK : 0 553 506072

First published in USA by Skylark Books,
a division of Bantam Doubleday Dell Publishing Group, Inc.

First publication in Great Britain

PRINTING HISTORY
Bantam edition published 1997

Set in 14/16pt Linotype New Century Schoolbook by
Phoenix Typesetting, Ilkley, West Yorkshire

Bantam Books are published by Transworld Publishers Ltd,
61–63 Uxbridge Road, Ealing, London W5 5SA,
in Australia by Transworld Publishers (Australia) Pty. Ltd,
15–25 Helles Avenue, Moorebank, NSW 2170,
and in New Zealand by Transworld Publishers (NZ) Ltd,
3 William Pickering Drive, Albany, Auckland.

Made and printed in Great Britain by
Cox & Wyman Ltd, Reading, Berks.

*I would like to express my special
thanks to Susan Korman
for her help in the
writing of this book.*

1
TWO GREAT IDEAS

Yeoowwwl!

As Corey Takamura hurried across her back garden to the stables, a howl filled the air.

Yeoowwwl!

The howl came again. Then a big, dark animal raced towards Corey and jumped up on her. She laughed as it began covering her face with kisses.

7

"I love you, too, Dracula," Corey told her dog. "But you have to get down. I'm already late for the Pony Tails meeting."

The big dog let out another of the weird-sounding howls that had given him his name. Dracula might *sound* spooky, but he was actually a very friendly dog.

After giving Corey a few more kisses, Dracula got down. He followed closely behind Corey as she continued across the yard to meet her two best friends, May Grover and Jasmine James.

Sometimes the Pony Tails got together at May or Jasmine's house. But today they were meeting inside the Takamuras' stables. It was the perfect place to meet for three animal lovers who called themselves the Pony Tails. Corey's mother was a veterinary surgeon. Dr Takamura – whom everybody called Doc Tock – always had an interesting assortment of animals staying in their stable block. This week the patients included an injured ferret, a basset hound named Ollie, and a litter of black kittens. Corey's pony, Sam, also lived there, and so did her pet goat, Alexander.

As Corey entered the big old stables, a smile spread across her face. She couldn't wait to tell her friends the news.

Every year one of the younger riders at Pine Hollow Stables gave a Halloween party. Pine Hollow was the stables where the three girls took lessons and went to Pony Club meetings. Corey had decided she would have this year's party. The best part was, she was going to make it a hayride.

The riders from Pine Hollow would love the idea – and Corey knew her two best friends would love it, too!

*   *   *

May and Jasmine were already sitting in an empty stall, waiting for Corey.

"What do you think Corey will say?" May asked Jasmine nervously. "Do you think she'll say it's a good idea?"

Jasmine tucked a strand of blond hair back into her pony-tail. "I'm not sure," she said. "It sounds fun. But you have to admit that inviting fifteen kids and fifteen ponies to Corey's house to go trick-or-treating is just a little bit crazy."

"It would be so much fun," said May. "Corey's mum is used to animals, so she won't mind the commotion. I bet Corey will think—"

"Think what?" a voice cut in.

May and Jasmine jumped as Corey stuck her head over the top of the stall.

"You scared me, Corey!" Jasmine said.

"Me too," said May.

"Sorry about that, you two," Corey

10

said. She opened the door of the stall and sat down beside her friends. Dracula bounded in after her. "So what will I think about what?" she asked.

May shot a nervous look at Jasmine.

"Tell her your idea, May," Jasmine said.

"Uh-oh. Another one of May's ideas?" Corey couldn't resist teasing her friend a little. Even May admitted that some of her ideas were crazy.

"You're going to love this idea, Corey," May said. "I've decided that you should have Pine Hollow's Halloween party at your house this year."

Corey stared at her friend, amazed. "I can't believe it!" she said. "That was my idea, too!"

"What?" Jasmine said. "You thought of that, too?"

Corey nodded. Actually she shouldn't have been too surprised

11

that she and May had come up with the same idea. With the Pony Tails, that happened all the time.

Shortly after Corey had moved into the house between May's and Jasmine's, the three girls had become best friends. One reason they liked each other so much was because they were all pony-crazy. Each girl owned her own pony, and she loved to ride that pony more than anything else in the world.

"Wait till you hear the rest of my idea," Corey went on. "I'm going to make the party a hayride! Won't that be fun?"

Corey babbled on for a few more minutes. Finally she realized she was the only one talking. Jasmine seemed interested in the hayride, but May was just sitting there, staring down at the straw.

"What's the matter, May?" Corey asked. "Did I say something that hurt your feelings?"

12

"Of course not, Corey," May said. She smiled, but Corey thought May still looked sad, or maybe disappointed.

"Don't you like my idea?" Corey asked.

"Having a hayride is a great idea, Corey," May began. "It's just that I had a different idea . . ."

"May wanted the party to be a trick-or-treating party," Jasmine said. "She thought we could invite riders *and* their ponies, and we could all go trick-or-treating on horseback."

"*Pony*back," May corrected her friend.

"Oh," Corey said as the words sank in. So that was why May had been so quiet.

For a few minutes there was an uncomfortable silence. Corey rubbed Dracula's ears. She didn't want to say so, but May's idea would never work. Doc Tock liked ponies almost as much as the Pony Tails did, but she

13

wouldn't like fifteen of them coming to her house all at once.

Finally Corey knew what to do.

"I've got it!" she shouted. "We can have a hayride *and* go trick-or-treating on ponyback!"

"What?" May stared at Corey. "Do both of them? I don't think so, Corey."

"We can have a hayride for the kids from Pine Hollow a couple of nights *before* Halloween," Corey explained. "And then on Halloween, the three of us can go trick-or-treating on ponyback ourselves. That would work — wouldn't it?"

May beamed. "Corey Takamura, you're a genius," she declared.

"No wonder we call you the most sensible member of the Pony Tails," Jasmine agreed.

Corey smiled happily. "You two stay right here," she said, jumping to her feet. "I'll go and get some paper and pencils and we can write down our ideas for the party."

"Hurry up," May said. "Halloween is only two weeks away. We'd better get started."

Corey swung open the stall door and rushed out into the corridor. She was so glad that everything had been worked out.

Suddenly something black and furry ran across the toe of her trainer.

"Aaagh!" Corey shrieked.

2
THE BLACK CAT

Corey's sharp cry echoed through the block.

May and Jasmine bolted out of the stall.

"Are you OK?" Jasmine asked.

Corey was standing in the aisle with an embarrassed look on her face. "I'm fine," she said. "One of the kittens ran by and scared me."

Just then the tiny black kitten

scooted out from between two bales of hay. It dashed past Corey again.

"Uh-oh, Corey," Jasmine teased her friend. "You know what it means when a black cat crosses your path."

"*Woooooo*." May made a ghost-like sound. "Bad luck," she added.

"You two have Halloween on your brains," Corey said with a grin. "Black cats aren't really bad luck. That's just a silly superstition."

Jasmine nodded. "It's as silly as believing that walking under a ladder is unlucky," she agreed.

"Or that breaking a mirror brings seven years of bad luck," May added.

"Right." Corey nodded. On the way to the house, she thought about the black cat that had made her shriek.

How could a tiny little kitten have spooked her like that?

An hour later, the Pony Tails had finished planning the Halloween party.

First they had decided they'd all be cowboys when they trick-or-treated for Halloween. Even though the Pony Tails rode English style, they were sure they could find or borrow Western gear, like boots and leather riding trousers called chaps.

"My mum has a bunch of cowboy hats," Jasmine said. "They'd be big enough to fit over our riding hats. And I bet she can make us some Western shirts."

The Pony Tails had also decided that the 'Haunted Hayride' two nights before Halloween would travel through the big field behind their houses. Along the route they could set up spooky things to scare the kids on the cart loaded with hay.

Jasmine was going to make fake tombstones. May wanted to dangle ghosts made out of sheets from the trees in the nearby woods.

"Maybe I can buy a CD with scary music," Corey said.

Her friends spoke at exactly the same time.

"Not *too* scary," Jasmine said.

"*Really* scary," May said.

Corey laughed. The Pony Tails might have a lot in common, but they certainly had differences, too!

"The most important thing on this list is finding a cart for the hay," Corey added. "I'd better get Mum to do that right away." She wrinkled her nose. "I hope it doesn't cost too much."

Suddenly May snapped her fingers. "We have a big old cart in our stables," she said. "I'm sure my dad will let us borrow it. And I bet Hank could pull it."

"That would be great," Corey said.

"I'll ask Dad tonight," May promised.

Corey checked the list one more time. They were inviting twelve riders from Pine Hollow to the party, as well as May and Jasmine's friend,

Joey Dutton. Joey used to live in Corey's house.

"I'll call Natalie, Jessica, Jackie and Amie," Corey said. "May, why don't you call Joey, Liam . . ." Her voice trailed off. "Did you two hear that?"

Jasmine shook her head. "Hear what?"

"That," Corey said as the sound came again. "I thought I heard something – like footsteps."

The girls were quiet for a few minutes, listening. As usual, there were plenty of animal noises in the stables. Jasmine could hear Alexander bleating and Dracula chasing a ball. Outside, Sam was shuffling his feet around in his paddock as he looked for clumps of grass to nibble on.

Jasmine turned back to Corey. "I can't hear anything," she told her friend. "Maybe it was the kittens again."

"Or Jack," May suggested. Jack

Henry was Doc Tock's assistant, and he was always working in the vet's office or inside the Takamuras' stable block.

"Maybe it was Jack," Corey said finally. "Or maybe I was just imagining things."

"This time *you've* got Halloween on your brain," Jasmine teased her.

"Definitely." Corey laughed, then said, "I'll invite Sarah Henry to the hayride."

"Who's that?" Jasmine asked.

"Jack's niece," Corey explained. "She's staying with Jack for a few weeks while her parents are away. She's been helping him with Mum's patients. She's a rider, too."

"I bet she'd want to go on a hayride," Jasmine said.

The girls divided the rest of the names of the riders on the party list. They had just finished when they heard one of May's sisters calling from next door.

"May!" Dottie yelled. "Dinnertime!"

"Coming!" May yelled back. "I think I'd better get going," she told her friends.

"Me too," Jasmine said. She rolled her eyes. "My dad's making tofu burgers for dinner. Yechh!"

Her friends nodded understandingly. Jasmine's parents were vegetarians. Jasmine liked most of what her parents cooked, but not tofu burgers. "See you two tomorrow," Jasmine added.

After her friends had gone, Corey spent a few more minutes in the stables visiting the basset hound and playing with the kittens. At six o'clock she hurried up to the house for dinner.

She couldn't wait to tell her mother about the Haunted Hayride. Spooking her friends from Pine Hollow was going to be so much fun!

3
SOMETHING SPOOKS SAM

"Sam's going really well today!" Jasmine called to Corey. "He hasn't missed one of your signals."

Corey nodded proudly. It was after school on Monday, and the Pony Tails were riding their ponies in the ring behind the Grovers' house. Mr Grover was a horse trainer and often used the big ring to train horses. When he wasn't using it, he let the Pony Tails ride there.

"Good boy, Sam." Corey patted her pony's neck. Sam's real name was Samurai because of the crescent-shaped blaze on his face, which looked like a samurai sword. He was a young pony and not as well trained as May's and Jasmine's ponies. But Corey had been working hard with him. That hard work was starting to pay off.

"Let's trot!" May called out.

Corey nudged Sam with her heels, and the pony obediently switched his pace from a walk to a trot. That was what the Pony Tails were working on with their ponies – paces. For the past hour they'd been practising the walk, trot, and canter.

"Good boy," Corey told Samurai. The two of them trotted evenly behind Jasmine and May.

Corey watched Jasmine try to get Outlaw to pick up speed by length-

26

ening his stride. Outlaw was feeling lazy, and that was showing up in his slow trot. Jasmine nudged the Welsh pony, and this time he followed her signal. Like Sam, Outlaw was usually a frisky pony and needed close attention.

Meanwhile May's pony, Macaroni, was trotting perfectly. Macaroni was a yellow pony, the colour of macaroni and cheese. Unlike the other two ponies, Macaroni almost never misbehaved.

The Pony Tails circled the ring at a trot for the third time.

"Hi, Corey!"

At the sound of her name, Corey looked to the right. A girl with short brown hair stood at the side of the ring, watching the Pony Tails ride.

"Hi, Sarah!" Corey yelled. It was Jack Henry's niece, Sarah. Corey slowed Sam to a walk and rode him over to Sarah.

"Sam's such a nice pony!" Sarah

patted Sam's soft nose. "Is he always this well behaved?"

Corey smiled and shook her head. "No way," she said. "He's a great pony, but he definitely has a mind of his own."

May and Jasmine joined them at the edge of the ring. Corey introduced them to Sarah.

"Corey's been working really hard with Sam," May piped up. "It's made a big difference."

"You should have seen him when Corey and her mum first moved in," Jasmine said. "Sam had a lot of problems getting used to his new home."

"That's true," Corey admitted. "He even ran away for a whole week once. But now our stables are his favourite place in the world. He acts like he's the king of the place."

"Well, you must be doing something right, Corey," Sarah told her. "Sam switches paces so smoothly. It looks like you're in total control."

"Corey told us you're a rider," May said. "Do you have your own pony?"

Sarah nodded, smiling happily. "That's why I'm waiting out here," she said. "My pony, Midnight, is going to be staying at Doc Tock's while my parents are away. Uncle Jack just went to pick her up."

"Her name's Midnight?" Jasmine smiled. "I bet she's a black pony."

Corey thought Sarah hesitated before she answered. "Actually she's a grey. Her first owner named her Midnight because she was born at the stroke of midnight."

"Oh." Jasmine nodded.

The Pony Tails and Sarah chatted about ponies and riding for a few more minutes. Sarah told them she belonged to Linton Pony Club.

May nodded. "I've seen Linton at lots of Pony Club events," she said.

That reminded Corey. 'We wanted to invite you to our Halloween party,"

29

she began. "We're having a hayride and—"

"I heard you talking about that the other day in the stables," Sarah cut in eagerly. "I'd love to come – it sounds really fun."

So it was Sarah she'd heard yesterday in the barn, Corey realized.

Just then Jack pulled up with a horse trailer.

"Hey, there's Midnight!" Sarah exclaimed. She ran over to greet Jack and her pony.

"Sarah must be so glad Midnight is here," Jasmine said. "I hate it when I go away and have to leave Outlaw behind."

Corey nodded. "It's really hard when I leave Sam to go to my dad's," she said. "I don't know what I'd do if you two didn't look in on him."

Corey's parents were divorced. She spent half the week with her mother and the other half with her father. At first it had been hard living in two different places, but she had got used to it.

"Hi, girls!" Jack called as the Pony Tails approached on their ponies. "I'm glad you met Sarah." He grinned. "I've already told her that you three are as pony-crazy as she is!"

The Pony Tails laughed. Corey didn't know Sarah very well. But she could already tell that Sarah loved her pony.

"Come on, Sarah," Jack said. He gestured with his thumb to the rear of the horse van. "Let's get Midnight unloaded. I'm sure you're eager to go riding with these girls."

"Why don't you tack up Midnight and meet us in the ring?" May asked.

"We're practising paces," Jasmine added.

"Uh . . ." Sarah blushed. "I can't go riding right now," she said.

"Do you have to get Midnight settled or something?" May asked.

"No." Sarah shook her head. "It's an

31

odd day," she said. "And I only ride Midnight on even days."

"What?" Corey had never heard anything so strange.

"Haven't you heard that greys are bad luck?" Sarah said, lowering her voice.

"Yes . . . but . . ." Corey knew that some people considered grey *horses* bad luck – especially grey racehorses. But she didn't know people believed that about ponies, too.

"That's ridiculous," May scoffed. "My family owns a grey horse named Hank. He's going to pull the hay cart at our party. He's always been *good* luck, not bad luck!"

Sarah looked embarrassed. "Well, I only ride Midnight on even days," she said. She scuffed at the ground with her foot.

Just then Jack called Sarah again. The Pony Tails looked at each other as she raced around to the back of the trailer.

32

"That's the strangest thing I ever heard," Jasmine said. "How can a girl think her own pony is bad luck?"

"I know," Corey agreed. "I . . ." She stopped talking and drew in a breath as Sarah led Midnight down the ramp.

Midnight was one of the prettiest ponies Corey had ever seen. The pony was a grey, as Sarah had said, with dark eyes and a silvery mane.

"Easy, boy," Corey said as Sam shuffled his feet nervously. "It's just a pony. Her name is Midnight."

"Wow." May was staring at Midnight, too. "She's beautiful."

"She looks so familiar," Jasmine said thoughtfully. "I know I've seen that pony before."

A few minutes later, Sarah led Midnight over to the Takamuras' stables. "See you later," she said, smiling as she passed the Pony Tails.

The girls waved. Corey was about

to turn Sam back to the Grovers' ring when something strange happened.

Suddenly Sam bucked. A surprised Corey flew off his back and landed on the ground with a thud.

"Whoa, Sam!" she yelled as her pony took off.

"We'll get him!" Jasmine cried. She and May sprang into action, chasing after Sam on their ponies.

Corey stood up, brushing the dust off the seat of her jodhpurs. Luckily she wasn't hurt. The really scary part was how suddenly Sam had acted up – his bad behaviour had come as a complete surprise.

A few minutes later, May led Sam back and then handed his reins to Corey.

"I guess Sam was being *too* good," May said with a grin. "He had to misbehave at least once today!"

"I suppose so," Corey agreed as she took the reins. "You're a naughty pony," she started to scold him. Then she noticed the wild look in Sam's eyes.

Sam wasn't being naughty – he was scared!

4
SARAH LISTENS IN

"It was the strangest thing," Corey told her mother as she served herself mashed potatoes at dinner that night. "I've never seen Sam act like that."

Doc Tock listened carefully while Corey described her pony's behaviour earlier that afternoon.

"Sometimes animal behaviour is mysterious, Corey," Doc Tock said with a shrug. "As a vet, there are

37

plenty of times when I can't understand my patients' behaviour." Then she sighed. "That goes for *human* behaviour, too."

"What do you mean, Mum?" Corey asked.

Her mother shook her head. "There's a new vet helping out at CARL. The director asked me to show him around so he can get to know the shelter."

Corey nodded. CARL was short for County Animal Rescue League, a local animal shelter that helped lots of sick and abandoned animals. Part of her mother's job as a vet involved taking care of the sick animals at CARL. Doc Tock had been doing it for as long as Corey could remember.

"Does the new vet misbehave like Sam?" Corey asked. "Is that why you can't work him out?"

Doc Tock smiled. "No," she said. "In fact, as far as I can tell, Jeff Helmer is a very good vet. The problem is me."

"You?" Corey said, surprised. "Why are *you* the problem?"

"This doesn't make me feel like a very nice person," Doc Tock admitted. "This guy hasn't really done anything wrong, but I just can't stand him. Everything he does gets on my nerves. He always wants to do things his way. If I have to spend one more day telling him why I do things a certain way, I'm going to scream."

Corey raised her eyebrows. It was strange to hear her calm, patient mother sound so frustrated. She had seen Doc Tock take care of all kinds of difficult animals and deal with their difficult owners. Only once or twice had Corey heard her mother lose her temper or act impatient while doing her job. It was very unlike her to say she disliked someone she worked with.

"Let's change the subject," Doc Tock said a minute later. "So how are the plans for the Haunted Hayride going?"

"Great, Mum," Corey said eagerly. They spent the rest of the meal talking about the Pony Tails' party plans.

"Hi, Mr Grover," Corey said into the phone. After dinner, Corey had called a few more riders to invite them to the party. Now she was calling May. "Is May there?"

"Just one moment, Corey," Mr Grover said. He put down the phone. Corey could hear him talking to May's older sister. "No, Dottie," he said. "Believe it or not, it isn't a boy, and it isn't for you."

Corey giggled. May's older sister, Dottie, was as boy-crazy as the Pony Tails were pony-crazy. Dottie spent most of her time on the phone talking to boys – or talking *about* them.

A second later, May picked up the phone. "Hello?"

Corey quickly told her about the calls she'd made so far. "Everybody can come," she reported. "But I still haven't reached Jackie Rogers. Her line was busy."

"Joey Dutton is coming, too," May said. "And so is Erin Mosley." She groaned. "I was hoping she'd say she had other plans."

Corey laughed. Erin Mosley was just about the only rider at Pine Hollow Stables the Pony Tails didn't like. Erin was stuck-up and liked to make trouble for the Pony Tails. Still, the Pony Tails had decided to invite her. It wouldn't be right to leave her out when all the other younger riders were invited.

May told Corey that Mr Grover had said he'd be glad to lend them both Hank and the cart. "Dad even said he would drive," May added.

"That's great!" Corey exclaimed. Mr Grover was so nice – he would be a perfect cart driver. And Hank was the perfect horse to pull the cart. Even though Hank was semi-retired now, the old grey was very steady.

"Hank loves being around kids," May said. "And nothing scares him, except for bad storms," she added.

The two girls talked about the party for a few more minutes. Then, as usual, their conversation turned back to their ponies.

"How was Sam when you put him in his stall?" May asked.

Corey sighed. "Well, he was glad to see Alexander," she began. Alexander was supposed to be Corey's pet goat. But by now everybody thought of him as Sam's pet. Ever since the little goat had moved into the stables, Sam had seemed content.

"But Sam was *not* happy about being untacked and put away for the night," Corey went on. "As soon as I shut the stall door, he started pawing the ground."

"Sam's still a young pony," May

reminded her. "He's much better behaved now, but he's going to act up from time to time."

"I suppose so," Corey replied. "But . . ." She thought back to the way he'd bucked that afternoon. His eyes had looked so wild.

"I still think something scared him today," she went on. "It was almost as if . . . Midnight spooked him or something."

"Corey Takamura!" May scolded her gently. "You're the most sensible member of the Pony Tails – remember? Don't tell me you really believe Sarah's pony is bad luck?"

"Nooo," Corey said slowly. "But don't you think it was a little strange that Sam bucked like that? It was right after Midnight passed by. And don't you think the way Sarah talked about Midnight is strange? She only rides her on even days!"

"I think it's silly," May said. "Grey ponies are beautiful – not unlucky."

By the time Corey hung up a few minutes later, she felt a lot better about Sam. Yesterday she'd heard footsteps in the stables. That had turned out to be Sarah helping Jack. She would find the explanation for Sam's odd behaviour, too.

Corey looked down at her list for Jackie Rogers's phone number. She was about to try Jackie again when she noticed someone standing in the doorway.

"You're right, Corey," Sarah said softly as she stepped into the kitchen. "Something did spook Sam today. It *was* Midnight."

5
IS MIDNIGHT BAD LUCK?

"What?" Corey jumped and dropped the phone receiver.

An embarrassed look crossed Sarah's face. "I didn't mean to listen to your conversation," she said. "I came inside to wait for Uncle Jack to finish up his chores. Then I heard what you were saying to your friend May."

An uneasy feeling settled in Corey's

stomach. Had Sarah heard *everything* she'd been saying to May? Including what she'd said about Sarah's acting strange?

"I thought you should know," Sarah went on. "Midnight did spook Sam this afternoon."

Corey shook her head. "Midnight didn't spook Sam," she said, remembering May's words. "Sam's still young. Sometimes he acts up."

"Sam was behaving perfectly until Midnight showed up," Sarah said. Her brown eyes looked very serious. "Listen, Corey," she added. "Sam's a great pony. I wouldn't want anything to happen to him."

Suddenly Corey felt worried. "What do you mean?"

Sarah sighed as she sat down at the table. "My parents bought Midnight for me about six months ago," she began. "Everything was great at first, but then at a Pony Club event I started having trouble."

46

"What kind of trouble?" Corey asked.

"Lots of different things," Sarah answered. "Finally I called Midnight's old owner, Mrs Lily. She's the one who told me that . . ." Tears sprang into Sarah's eyes. "She said Midnight is bad luck," she finished in a hoarse voice. "Mrs Lily also said Midnight spooks other ponies and horses."

Corey stared at the other girl. Did Sarah actually believe what she was saying?

"Come on, Sarah," Corey said finally. "That's just a silly superstition about grey ponies."

Sarah shook her head. "It's true, Corey. That's why I only ride Midnight on even days. That's what Mrs Lily told me to do."

"If Midnight's this much trouble, why do you keep her?" Corey asked. "It doesn't make sense."

Sarah looked Corey straight in

the eye. "I love her," she answered.

That stopped Corey short. She loved her pony too, even though Sam did lots of naughty things.

Outside, Corey heard Jack start his pickup truck.

Sarah heard it, too. "I'd better go." She stood up from the table, then glanced down at Corey. "If I were you, I'd watch Sam closely," she warned. "A few months before I bought her, Midnight spooked a Thoroughbred so badly, he never let another rider on his back. That's why Mrs Lily had to sell Midnight."

"Come on, Sarah," Corey said, shaking her head. "That can't be true. And even if it was true, what could I do about Midnight's spooking Sam anyway?"

"Mrs Lily says there's one way to protect a pony that's being spooked," Sarah answered. "Tie seven heads of garlic together and throw them around the pony's neck."

48

That was even crazier than the idea of a haunted pony!

Corey was about to tell Sarah that. But when she looked up again, Sarah was gone.

The next morning after breakfast, Corey went out to the stables to feed Sam. She also wanted to say goodbye to him. After school she was leaving to stay at her father's for a few days.

As she went into the barn, Dracula howled a greeting at her.

"Morning, Dracula," Corey answered. She patted his head while his tail wagged.

As she approached Sam's stall, Corey could hear her pony stamping and shuffling around nervously.

"What's the matter, boy?" Corey asked. She reached out to stroke his nose, but Sam turned away. He wouldn't even take his favourite treat, a juicy red apple.

Alexander bleated softly and scampered over to Corey.

"What's the matter with Sam?" Corey asked the goat.

The baby goat nuzzled her hand in reply. If Sam didn't want the apple, then he was going to take it. She let Alexander have it. He munched happily.

Corey stared at her unhappy pony. A hollow feeling grew in the bottom of her stomach. She was pretty sure that Sarah had been talking nonsense the night before. But now Sarah's words played back inside Corey's head.

Sam's a great pony . . . I wouldn't want anything to happen to him . . .

There's no such thing as a pony who spooks other ponies, Corey reminded herself.

Corey spent the next few minutes calmly talking to Sam. By the time she was ready to leave, he had relaxed a little, and so had she.

On her way out of the stables, Corey

spotted Midnight standing alone in her stall. The pony gazed at Corey with her big dark eyes.

"Corey?" May yelled into the barn.

"Are you in here?" Jasmine called.

"Over here," Corey answered.

When May and Jasmine approached, they saw Corey staring at Midnight. Corey told her friends what Sarah had said the night before.

"Don't tell me you believe it, Corey!" Jasmine said. "First Sarah says Midnight's bad luck because she's grey. And now she's saying her pony *spooks* other ponies and horses?"

"I've never heard anything so crazy!" May chimed in.

"It *sounds* crazy," Corey agreed. "But Sam was still acting nervous this morning, and I can't work out why."

All three members of the Pony Tails looked at Midnight.

There's definitely something different about Sarah's pony, Corey thought. Midnight stood there calmly, and carefully watched the Pony Tails' every move. In the dark stables, her grey coat was so light, it almost seemed to glow.

"We'd better get going," Jasmine said a minute later. "The bus will be here soon."

With a sigh, Corey reached down to pick up the backpack she was bringing to her father's. She hated to leave Sam behind – especially when he was acting so odd.

The only good part about leaving was knowing that May and Jasmine would check on Sam and take good care of him. Still, Corey wished she could stay and take care of Sam herself.

6
"WELL DONE, COREY!"

On Saturday morning Corey's father dropped her off at Pine Hollow for the Pony Club meeting. Inside the tack room, Max was starting the meeting. He opened every meeting by saying the same thing.

"Horse Wise, come to order!"

Horse Wise was the name of Pine Hollow's Pony Club. Corey was glad today's meeting was a mounted one.

That meant the members would be riding their horses or ponies instead of talking about them. Unmounted meetings were always interesting, but they were never as much fun as mounted ones.

Corey sat on the floor next to Jasmine and May. They smiled at her, then quickly turned to face Max. They didn't want their riding instructor to catch them talking.

"We're going to be working with cavalletti poles," Max explained. "Everybody's familiar with them, aren't they?"

Erin Mosley's hand shot up into the air.

"Oh, great," May groaned softly. "What does Miss Know-it-all have to say today?"

"Cavalletti are one of the most popular pieces of training equipment," Erin said, tossing her curly blond hair proudly.

"That's right, Erin," Max told her.

54

"These poles are a great help when you're schooling horses. Today we're going to be using them in our trotting exercises to help our ponies keep long and even strides. Outside we'll break up into small groups and . . ."

Corey was glad to hear that the riders would be working on trotting. She and Sam had been working on this pace for the last few weeks. She knew the extra practice would be a big help.

When Max was finished with his instructions, everybody stood up.

"Sam's waiting for you in his usual borrowed stall," May told Corey. "We'll meet you in the outdoor ring."

Corey hurried off to collect Sam, thinking about how lucky she was to live next door to the Grovers. Mr Grover was the one who brought the girls' ponies to the mounted meetings. When he was too busy to drive the ponies over in his horsebox, the girls could ride stable ponies. But it wasn't the same as riding their own.

Corey greeted Sam, and he nickered. After three whole days of being apart, Corey and her pony were glad to see each other. Sam even stood patiently while Corey tightened the girth on his saddle.

When Sam was tacked up, Corey led him to the outdoor ring. Most of the other riders were already there.

First Corey and Sam practised walking over the cavalletti poles. Then she asked Sam to trot. Gradually, she added more poles.

To her delight, Sam performed perfectly.

Even Max noticed.

"Well done, Corey," he complimented her. Then he made the rest of the riders stop what they were doing to watch Sam and Corey.

"This is exactly what I like to see," Max said to the members of Horse Wise. "Corey has been very patient with her pony. She's worked up to the

56

trot very slowly. She's also been careful not to add extra poles too soon."

Corey blushed. Max had complimented her before. But he had never made her an example in front of everyone.

"In other words," the riding instructor went on, "she has the good sense to respect her pony and his special training needs."

"While showing him that she's in charge," May called out. She gave Corey a thumbs-up.

"That's right. Well done, Corey," Max said again.

Max's words made Corey feel very proud.

Inside the stable, Corey hugged Sam.

"I'm going to give you an extra-special grooming today," she promised. "That's because you did so well. Then you can rest while May, Jasmine, and I help with some stable chores."

A tradition at Pine Hollow was that the riders pitched in. There were a lot of jobs that needed to be done around the busy stables. Asking riders to help was one way Max and his mother, Mrs Reg, managed to keep the riders' costs down.

Corey untacked Sam, then found her grooming kit. She pulled out her hoofpick and went to work. She knew that picking out a pony's hooves was an important part of grooming. If a stone got stuck in Sam's hoof, it could injure him, or even worse, make him go lame.

She was brushing Sam's coat when Amie and Jackie hurried over.

"We can't wait for your party," Jackie said. "Are you really going to make it a *haunted* hayride?"

Corey nodded. "We've got lots of spooky stuff planned," she said. "And after the hayride we're going to have a bonfire and tell ghost stories."

Amie grinned. "Oh, good. I love ghost stories!"

Suddenly it seemed as if everyone wanted to talk about the party. While Corey was grooming Sam, several other riders came up. Every one of them said they were looking forward to the party. It made Corey feel even more glad the Pony Tails had decided to have a hayride.

After lunch, it was time for the Pony Tails to start the stable chores. The first chore was cleaning the tack in the tack room. Polishing metal stirrups and bits and rubbing down saddles with soap wasn't Corey's favourite job. It wasn't too bad when her best friends did it with her.

As the Pony Tails worked, Jasmine told Corey that Sam had been good while Corey was at her father's.

"Even around Midnight?" Corey asked.

"Well . . ." Jasmine hesitated.

"Midnight wasn't in her stall when we checked on Sam one time. Then another time, they were both in the paddock, but they weren't grazing near each other."

"Corey," May said sternly. "Forget about Midnight. She's not bad luck, and she's not spooking Sam."

"OK, OK," Corey said. She grinned sheepishly. "You two are right. Even Max said how great Sam's doing."

"Right. The one to worry about is Sarah," May said.

Corey put down the jar of metal polish. "What do you mean?"

May and Jasmine exchanged looks.

"The other day we asked her if she wanted to ride with us," Jasmine explained. "She said she couldn't—"

"Because it was another odd-numbered day!" May chimed in. "Can you believe her? And get this. Yesterday, before she rode Midnight around the ring, we watched her tack up. Before she put the saddle on

60

Midnight's back, she walked around her three times. Then she said, 'Hocus pocus, sucoh, sucop.'"

"What?" Corey wrinkled her nose. "*Sucoh, sucop*? What does that mean?"

"It's *hocus pocus* spelled backwards!" Jasmine exclaimed. "That's what she said that lady, Mrs Lily, told her to do before tacking up."

May and Jasmine started to giggle.

Corey couldn't giggle with them. She was still too worried about Sam and Sarah and her superstitions, no matter how silly May and Jasmine made them sound.

7
THE GOOD-LUCK HORSESHOE

At four o'clock, it was time for the Pony Tails to go home. May's father would be arriving soon to pick up the girls and their ponies.

May and Jasmine were ready first.

"We'll meet you outside, Corey," May yelled. "We're going to wait in the drive for my dad."

"OK," Corey called back. "I'll be

there in a minute." She hurried to Sam's stall to untie him.

"Time to go home, boy," she said, clipping on his lead rein.

On her way out of the stable, something caught Corey's eye.

It was the good-luck horseshoe, which hung on the wall above the mounting block.

When Corey had started riding at Pine Hollow, the horseshoe was one of the first things May and Jasmine had told her about. Every rider was supposed to touch the horseshoe before a mounted Pony Club meeting. According to May and Jasmine, no rider who had touched the horseshoe had ever been seriously hurt. Corey had never really thought about it before, but in a way, the horseshoe was a superstition, too.

"*Staring* at the horseshoe won't do you any good," a voice said suddenly.

Corey turned around. Mrs Reg,

Max's mother, was standing there, smiling.

"You have to *touch* it," the older woman added. "The horseshoe can't bring you luck unless you rub it."

"I know," Corey nodded. "May says it's like magic."

Mrs Reg's blue eyes twinkled. "Then again, maybe it's just a silly superstition that everybody's afraid to break."

Corey stared at her, surprised. Mrs Reg had done it again. Somehow Max's mother always seemed to know what riders were thinking about – sometimes even before they knew it themselves!

Corey turned back to the horseshoe. "Why do people believe in superstitions anyway, Mrs Reg?" she asked.

Mrs Reg shrugged. "For some people they make new or unfamiliar situations less frightening."

"Do you believe in them?" asked Corey.

"The way I see it, most superstitions are just plain foolish," Mrs Reg answered. "But a few of them are harmless. Like the good-luck horseshoe. It certainly doesn't hurt anybody to touch it. And it reminds riders to be careful."

A horn tooted in the drive outside.

"That's Mr Grover," Corey said. "See you later, Mrs Reg."

Corey took one last look at the good-luck horseshoe.

Did it really protect the riders? she wondered.

She wished she knew the answer.

The Pony Tails chattered about the hayride all the way home from Pine Hollow.

"I finished making the tombstones for the graveyard last night," Jasmine said. "Wait till you two see them. I painted them with glow-in-the-dark paint."

"Terrific," said May.

"My mum and I are going to work on a shopping list tonight," Corey said. "We're going to make some spider biscuits and some other Halloween snacks."

"I'm still working on the ghosts to hang from the trees," May said. "Believe it or not, my sisters offered to help us on the night of the party." She giggled. "They're very good at scaring people, you know!"

"Did you buy the CD, Corey?" Jasmine asked.

Corey nodded. "Wait till you hear the music – it's pretty spooky."

"Hey, you girls have thought of everything," Mr Grover said from the front seat.

"The Pony Tails always come prepared," May declared.

A few minutes later, Mr Grover

stopped the horsebox in the Grovers' drive. Corey followed May and Jasmine as they hopped out of the box and ran around to the back.

"We're home, boys!" May called to the three ponies.

Macaroni was the first to come down the ramp. As usual, he walked down with no fuss.

But when Jasmine tried to lead Outlaw out of the horsebox, he tossed his head stubbornly.

Uh-oh, Corey thought, Outlaw's about to make trouble.

Then Outlaw looked at Macaroni standing calmly outside. That was all he needed. He practically trotted out of the lorry and over to his friend's side.

Corey laughed. Sometimes the Pony Tails' ponies seemed to be as good friends as their owners were!

"Your turn, Sam," Corey told her pony. She climbed into the horsebox and untied Sam. He refused to budge.

"Come on, boy," Corey murmured. Her friends were already leading their ponies over to the Grovers' paddock. "You've been so good all day. Don't make trouble now."

Sam stomped one hoof and blew air through his nose.

"I think you're not going to do what I'm asking you to do," Corey sighed. She headed down the ramp alone.

"May! Jasmine!" she called to her friends. "Can you . . ."

Corey's words trailed off. She spotted something near her mum's stable block. Sarah was leading Midnight around the paddock.

A shiver went up Corey's spine.

Is that why Sam is being so stubborn? she wondered. Is he scared of Midnight?

Just then Sam let out a loud, pitiful whinny.

"What's the matter, Corey?" May yelled as she and Jasmine raced over. Their ponies were tied to the fence

69

around the Grovers' paddock. "Won't Sam come out?"

Corey shook her head. She was still staring at Sarah and Midnight.

May looked in the same direction.

"Corey," May said warningly. "This doesn't mean that Midnight spooked Sam."

"You *always* have problems unloading Sam," Jasmine reminded Corey.

Corey didn't say anything as she and her friends tried to get Sam out of the horsebox. She was worried about Sam. What if everything Sarah had told her was true? What if Midnight *had* spooked Sam? And what if Midnight spooked him again, the way he'd spooked the Thoroughbred at his last home? What if she couldn't ever ride him again?

She couldn't bear the thought.

A few minutes later the Pony Tails managed to get Sam down the ramp, but not without a fight. The three of them practically had to drag Sam outside and into the stable block. By the time Sam was settled in his stall for the night, Corey had made up her mind. Just as Mrs Reg had said, some superstitions couldn't hurt.

Corey was going to make a garlic necklace for her pony.

8
THE GARLIC NECKLACE

The next morning Corey and her mother went to the supermarket to buy food for the party.

When they got home, the phone was ringing in the kitchen.

Doc Tock picked up the receiver. "Hello?" she said. "Oh, hi, Jeff. How are you?"

Corey watched her mother's face as she talked to the new vet at CARL.

"No, that's *not* what I do." Doc Tock frowned. "Champ gets fed twice a day, not once." She listened for a second, then snapped, "Oh, I suppose so . . ."

When she hung up the phone, she sighed with frustration. "What is it with that man?" she burst out.

Corey smiled sympathetically. "It sounds like Dr Helmer's driving you crazy, Mum."

"He is," Doc Tock said. "He acts like he's been around CARL for ever. He doesn't seem to respect any of my systems for treating the animals."

Doc Tock continued to complain about Jeff Helmer while they unpacked the groceries.

Corey unloaded the bag filled with the ingredients for the spider biscuits: plain wafers, vanilla icing, and black liquorice. She also unpacked a jar of marshmallow spread, which would get smeared across toast cut out in spooky shapes for the 'ghost toast'.

Suddenly Doc Tock stopped talking

about Dr Helmer. She held up a plastic bag filled with garlic. "You never told me, honey. What's the garlic for?"

Corey felt her face turn red. "I'm, uh, making a garlic necklace."

"Is that to keep away the vampires during the hayride?" Doc Tock asked, laughing. "Hey, this is going to be a terrific party. You girls have such great ideas."

"Thanks, Mum." Corey pretended to laugh along with her mother as she took the garlic and shoved it into her backpack. She wanted to tell Doc Tock the truth. She wanted to say that she was planning to make a garlic necklace to protect Sam from Midnight. Corey knew her mother would tell her she was just being silly. It was easier to just let Doc Tock think the garlic was for the party.

Corey had decided not to tell May and Jasmine about the necklace, either. For now it would be her secret.

As soon as they had finished unpacking the groceries, Corey grabbed her backpack and hurried upstairs. She dumped the garlic on her desk, then searched her drawers for a ball of string.

For the next few days, Corey managed to stop worrying so much about Sam. It helped that she spent most of the week at her father's flat. By the time she returned to her mother's on Thursday, there was plenty to do for the Haunted Hayride.

On Friday afternoon the Pony Tails met in the Grovers' stables.

"Ready to decorate?" May asked.

Corey nodded and took a roll of orange crepe paper from May. The girls were getting the hay cart ready for the next night. Corey had the orange crepe paper, May had a roll of black crepe paper. They wound it around the cart and taped it in place. Jasmine was in charge of fastening scary pictures of witches and skeletons to the sides of the cart.

"It looks great!" May announced when they had finished. Jasmine and Corey quickly agreed.

The Pony Tails' next job was to load up the cart with bales of hay. May stood on top of it while Jasmine and Corey lifted the bales up to her. The bales were heavy, and it was hard work.

Corey was thinking they would never finish when Sarah stuck her head into the Grovers' stable. "Need help?" she asked.

"Yes, please!" May told her. "Come on up."

Sarah hopped on top of the cart. Things went much more swiftly after that. Together May and Sarah arranged the bales of hay around the edges of the cart. Then the four of them covered the floor of the cart with loose hay.

While they worked, Sarah told

77

them more about her Pony Club.

"Next month we're putting on a holiday show to raise some money. I'm supposed to be in the dressage competition." She sighed. "I hope it's held on an even day."

May and Jasmine exchanged looks. But Corey was impressed. Dressage was a form of riding that required a lot of skill and precision. She hadn't seen Sarah ride much, but if she and her pony could handle dressage movements, they must be pretty good together.

A few minutes later Sarah said she had to go.

Corey thanked her for her help.

"It was fun," Sarah said, smiling. "I can't wait for the party – Midnight and I are going home afterwards. My parents will be back by tomorrow night."

The Pony Tails waved as Sarah left the stables.

"I'm glad she helped," May said.

"We'd still be working if she hadn't come over."

Jasmine was quiet. Suddenly she turned to Corey.

"I've just remembered!" she declared. "That's where I saw Midnight!"

"Where?" Corey asked.

"Remember that big Pony Club rally a few months ago?" Jasmine began.

"Yes." Corey nodded. Jasmine was talking about a big rally Horse Wise had attended, along with several other local Pony Clubs.

"I think Midnight was the pony that threw a rider from Linton Pony Club," Jasmine went on. "I don't think the rider was Sarah – this girl had long blond hair."

"Right." May suddenly remembered. "Emma O'Rourke. She broke her arm, didn't she?"

Jasmine nodded.

Corey could remember the rally,

but not the accident. The event had been held right around the time she'd moved and started riding at Pine Hollow. Back then, she was still trying to learn about Horse Wise, her own Pony Club. She hadn't paid much attention to the riders from other clubs.

May smiled. "I wonder if Emma made a mistake and rode Midnight on an odd day," she said.

Jasmine giggled. "Maybe she forgot to say 'Hocus pocus, sucop, sucoh,' before she got on."

Corey listened to her friends talk about Midnight and Sarah. She felt more and more nervous.

That was what Sarah had meant when she said Midnight had caused trouble at a Pony Club event. Midnight had thrown Sarah's friend. That was one of the reasons Sarah believed Midnight was bad luck.

As soon as she got home that afternoon, Corey raced up to her room. She got down on her hands and knees and checked under her bed.

The garlic necklace looked a little dusty, but it was lying just where she'd put it earlier in the week.

"Don't worry, Sam," Corey whispered as she pulled it out. "I'm not going to let *anything* happen to you tomorrow night."

9
ALL ABOARD THE
HAUNTED HAYRIDE

"Howdy, pardner!" a boy in a bat costume said as Corey opened the door. "I've come to suck your blood!"

"Great costume, Billy," Corey said, laughing. "Come on in. Everybody's in the living room."

Billy flapped his inflatable bat wings and followed Corey into the Takamuras' house. Most of the riders from Pine Hollow had already arrived for the haunted hayride.

Doc Tock was trying to keep two of them under control.

"That's enough, boys," she called to Joey and Liam. Joey had on a pirate costume, and Liam was dressed as a knight. For the past ten minutes, they had been trying to stab each other with their plastic swords.

"Sorry about that, Doc Tock," Joey said, putting down his pirate sword.

Doc Tock smiled. "I don't want anyone walking the gangplank before the hayride," she joked.

The Pony Tails were dressed alike in their cowboy costumes. They each had on chaps, Western riding boots, tall cowboy hats, and shirts that Mrs James had decorated with beads and fringe so that they'd look Western.

Erin Mosley had come as a princess, in a long white gown and a sparkling tiara. Sarah was dressed in a bright orange pumpkin suit.

"The hayride is going to be so great," May whispered in Corey's ear. "Everybody's really excited."

Corey nodded. "I hope it doesn't rain," she whispered back. "The weatherlady on TV said there's going to be a thunderstorm tonight."

"No, it won't," May said. She showed Corey her crossed fingers. "This is for good luck."

A few minutes later May pointed out the window. "He's here!" she shouted. "My dad's here with the cart."

Everybody scrambled to get their coats and head out the door.

"All aboard the Haunted Hayride Express!" Mr Grover called.

For the occasion, May's father had got dressed up in his own costume – flannel shirt and overalls, complete with a red-and-white bandanna and a monster mask.

Mr Grover and Jack helped the kids climb on to the cart. Liam and Joey

85

were the first aboard. The two boys immediately raced for the back and started throwing hay everywhere.

"Stop it!" Erin cried. She brushed hay from her tiara and gave the boys a nasty look.

May giggled. "She's afraid they'll ruin her princess costume."

Jasmine rolled her eyes. "Wouldn't that be a shame," she muttered.

Minutes later, everyone was seated. The hay throwing had stopped – at least for now.

"We're off," Mr Grover shouted. He flicked the long black reins gently against Hank's back, and with a lurch, the hay cart left the Takamuras' yard.

The Pony Tails exchanged excited looks.

The Haunted Hayride had begun!

The cart began to circle the field. Corey glanced up at the sky. Dark clouds slid across the moon. The only other light came from the row of paper-bag lanterns the Pony Tails had placed along the route.

"Look at that!" Amie shouted. She pointed to a tombstone about fifteen metres ahead.

May, Corey and Jasmine grinned.

"It looks great, Jasmine," May whispered.

And it did. The tombstone was made out of cardboard and painted neon green. Eerie shadows from a nearby lantern flickered across it.

Amie and the other riders gasped as they read the words painted there.

HERE LIES THE BODY OF
JOEY DUTTON
VICTIM OF A VAMPIRE BAT

"Hey, that's me!" Joey said, jumping up from his seat. He pulled off his pirate's eye-patch so that he could see better.

"Guess you got pushed overboard, matey," Liam said, chuckling.

"Very funny," Joey said back.

A second later, the two boys were throwing hay again.

The cart drew close to another tombstone glowing in the dark. This time Jackie read the words painted on it aloud.

HERE LIES LIAM O'NEILL
PONY CLUB RIDER
FRIEND OF ALL ANIMALS
— ESPECIALLY THE
LION THAT ATE HIM

"I think you spoke too soon, Liam," May said.

"That's right," Joey said, throwing more hay at his friend.

The group passed a few more tombstones; then Mr Grover turned the cart into the woods at the far end of the field.

A cloud covered the moon. Suddenly the dark night grew even blacker. The riders' voices dropped to whispers as they looked around nervously.

"What's happening?" Erin Mosley murmured.

Corey flicked on the CD player that was hidden near her feet.

A low moan filled the air, growing louder and louder.

Amie clutched Jackie's arm, and Natalie's eyes looked as round as a full moon.

"Aaaaahhhhh!"

Erin Mosley's scream ripped through the dark night.

The other riders screamed, too, as an enormous ghost swooped down over the cart, grazing their heads.

"That was perfect!" May whispered to Corey and Jasmine. "Dottie did it right on time!"

Over their heads, May's sister Dottie was perched in the branches of an oak tree. Her latest boyfriend, Peter, was with her. He dangled another ghost over the riders' heads.

The riders screamed at the top of their lungs, loving every minute of it.

"Look over there!" Billy shouted a few seconds later. "A body's hanging from a noose!"

The cart continued around the field, encountering horror after horror.

Corey couldn't believe how calm and steady Hank remained. Lots of other horses would have been upset by all the spooky surprises – and a cart full of shrieking kids. But Hank didn't seem to notice. Instead he plodded along, obediently following Mr Grover's instructions.

Corey sat under the heavy blankets between Jasmine and May. She sighed happily. It was fun to be out here, terrifying all her friends.

Jasmine was thinking the same thing. "I'm glad you thought of a hayride, Corey."

"It's almost as fun as trick-or-treating on horseback," May teased her.

"*Pony*back, not horseback, May," Corey teased back. "And we'll be doing that two days from now – remember?"

"I can't wait!" May declared.

Finally the hay cart came to the last fright on the Haunted Hayride.

"Hey!" Liam yelled. "A headless horseman!" Everybody turned to see the dummy the Pony Tails had made and stuck on top of May's old rocking horse.

It wore Mr Grover's jeans, an old flannel shirt, and a straw hat. The Pony Tails had spilled ketchup all over the top of his shirt, where the missing head was supposed to be.

"Cool," Joey cried. "Blood!"

A few minutes later, the cart turned into the Takamuras' yard.

The riders groaned.

"The hayride is over already?" Amie said.

91

"Not yet," Corey reminded her friends. "We still have the bonfire and ghost stories."

Suddenly there was a low, faraway rumble. It was thunder.

10
GHOST STORIES

In the Takamuras' back garden a bonfire glowed brightly.

"Whoa, Hank," Mr Grover called, and the cart came to a stop.

"Welcome back!" Doc Tock called to the riders. "Did you have a good time?"

"Terrific," Natalie said.

"You should have seen the ghosts,

Doc Tock!" Jackie added. "They were so scary."

"So was that blood, or whatever it was, dripping down the tree," Erin said. She made a disgusted face. "We didn't do anything like this at *my* Halloween party."

As usual, Erin was jealous of something the Pony Tails had done. Corey did her best to ignore the snooty girl's comment.

After all the riders had jumped off the cart, Corey thanked Mr Grover. "It was lots of fun. You and Hank did a great job."

Mr Grover removed his mask and smiled at her. "Hank's as steady as they come," he said. "He did the hard work. I just came along for the fun." He glanced over at the bonfire. The riders were gathering around while Doc Tock handed out cups of steaming cocoa and plates heaped with ghost toast and spider cookies.

"That cocoa really looks good," Mr

Grover said. "I think I'll park old Hank in your stable block and get myself a cup."

Corey took her own cocoa and sat down near the fire next to May and Jasmine. She was chatting with her friends until a sound from the stables sent a shiver up her spine.

It was Sam's loud whinny.

Corey glanced over at the stables. From where she was sitting, she couldn't see Sam. Through the open door she could see Midnight poking her head over the top of her stall. She was tacked up for her ride home in the trailer. The pony was looking at Hank. The old horse was standing in the wide aisle, still hitched to the cart.

Corey reached into the pocket of her coat. Her fingers brushed against the garlic necklace. She hoped she wouldn't need it. She was ready, just in case.

A few minutes later Doc Tock stood

up. "OK, everybody. It's time for ghost stories."

Liam and Joey did a high five.

"All right!" Liam said.

As she watched the two boys, Jasmine looked worried. "I hope they don't get too carried away," she said. "I don't really like scary stories."

"I do," May said, eagerly rubbing her hands. "Stevie Lake told me a really good one last week at Pine Hollow." She jumped to her feet. "I've got one, Doc Tock," she said. "Can I go first?"

"Sure," Doc Tock answered.

Corey watched May as she began her story in a hushed voice. The light from the fire cast an eerie glow across her face.

Once there was a rider named Cassie who always wore a bandanna around her neck. It was a beautiful purple bandanna, which she wore every day – no matter what.

One day she met another rider named Joe. "Why do you always wear that bandanna around your neck?" he asked. Cassie shook her head. "I'll tell you when the time is right," she said.

Eventually the two riders fell in love, and soon they got married.

"Now will you tell me why you wear the bandanna?" Joe asked Cassie.

Again she shook her head. "I'll tell you when the time is right," she said.

The two riders grew old together. They rode their horses every day, and every day Cassie still wore the purple bandanna.

One day Cassie grew ill. She knew she was dying. She called her husband to her bedside.

Suddenly May's voice dropped to a whisper.

"It is time, my love," she said. Slowly she untied the bandanna and . . .

May looked up at the group of riders. By now they were hanging on her every word.

And as Cassie untied the purple bandanna, her head fell off!

Joey and Liam howled with laughter. All the other riders loved May's story, too. Even Jasmine.

It sounds about right that Stevie Lake told that story to May, Corey thought, smiling. Stevie was an older rider at Pine Hollow with a really weird sense of humour. She was always telling jokes and funny stories to the younger riders.

"Can I go next?" Jackie yelled.

"Sure," Doc Tock replied.

Jackie started to speak. The wind rustled the trees. A loud whinny came from inside the stables.

Corey thought she'd better check on Sam.

Jasmine reached over to squeeze Corey's hand. "Stop worrying," she whispered. "Sam is fine."

Corey smiled, hoping Jasmine was right. "OK," she said. "Thanks."

Corey didn't look at the stables again until Jackie had finished her story. Midnight was still standing calmly in her stall. But Hank didn't look calm at all. The old grey horse was champing on his bit, and rattling his harness.

"May!" Corey whispered. Her friend was listening to Natalie tell a funny story about a vampire who liked tomato juice.

"May!" Corey whispered again.

"Shhh, Corey," May hissed back. "I want to hear this."

Then Corey saw something even more frightening. Inside the stables Hank's eyes were wide with fear, and he was tossing his head.

Oh, no! Corey thought, jumping to her feet.

Midnight hadn't spooked Sam tonight. She'd spooked Hank!

11
HANK SPOOKS

Corey raced over to the stables. She had to reach Hank before it was too late!

Hank pawed at the ground frantically. Then he shook the harness again. Corey could see that he wanted to get away from the Takamuras' stables – and fast!

"Easy, boy," Corey said. With one hand she stroked the horse's face.

With the other hand she grabbed hold of the garlic necklace in her pocket and tossed it up over Hank's neck.

"It's OK now, Hank," Corey said softly. "The necklace will protect you. Midnight can't spook you any more."

Just then Sarah rushed toward Corey. "Is Hank OK?" she asked. "I saw you put the garlic necklace on him, and I thought—"

"Hank's fine now," Corey cut in. "But a few minutes ago he seemed pretty spooked."

Sarah looked surprised. "Good thing you had the garlic necklace ready," she said. "I didn't think you believed me."

Corey nodded. "I made it for Sam," she explained. "I wasn't expecting to use it on Hank."

Suddenly Sarah's eyes went wide. She pointed at Hank.

As Corey faced the Grovers' horse, her heart skipped a beat. Hank was still tossing his mane and trying to shake free of the harness.

Oh, no, Corey thought. What's happening now?

Boom!

A furious clap of thunder interrupted Corey's thoughts.

"That's it, everybody," Doc Tock called out to the riders gathered around the fire. "Let's move the party into the house."

From the back of the stables, Dracula howled. A strong wind blew. The riders jumped up and began to gather their things. Then rain began to fall.

Hank pawed at the ground. Corey was afraid the horse might rear when he let out a high-pitched whinny instead. A split second later, the frightened horse bolted. As he tore out of the stables, the empty hay cart pounded the ground behind him.

"Whoa, Hank!" Mr Grover shouted

as Hank raced past the group of riders. "Come back, boy!"

But the spooked horse didn't listen. Hank kept on going, running towards the dark field behind Corey's house as fast as his legs could carry him.

"Go after him, Dad!" May shouted.

Sarah had already thought of that. Without a word, she threw open the stall door, jumped on Midnight's back, and dug in her heels.

"No, Sarah!" Doc Tock shouted as she realized what was happening. "You can't ride out there! Not with a thunderstorm coming."

Sarah didn't hear Doc Tock. She leaned over her pony, urging her to pick up speed. They raced away from the stables, chasing Hank into the open field behind the Pony Tails' houses.

Mr Grover was the next one to spring into action. "I'll go after her!" he yelled. He ran next door to get

Dobbin, another of the Grovers' horses.

"Everybody get into the stable block – now!" Corey's mum ordered again.

Sensing that Doc Tock meant business, the riders quickly followed her instructions.

Jasmine came over and squeezed Corey's hand. "Don't worry," she said. "Hank won't get very far. He's an old horse."

"And the cart will slow him down," May added. "Sarah and my dad will catch up to him soon."

Corey nodded. But she still felt worried – especially when she saw lightning flash in the distance.

12
THE RESCUE

Rain pounded the roof of the stables.

Corey looked outside for the hundredth time. There was still no sign of Hank, or of Sarah and Mr Grover. The rain was coming down so hard, she couldn't imagine how Sarah could see where she was going on Midnight. And how would Mr Grover ever find the two of them and Hank?

"Thanks so much, Doc Tock and Corey," Amie Connor's mother said as she arrived to pick up Amie and Jackie. She held a big golf umbrella over the girls' heads. "It sounds like everybody had a wonderful time on the hayride."

"You're welcome," Doc Tock replied. "See you soon."

Corey waved goodbye to the last of the guests. May and Jasmine had gone inside the Takamuras' house to start cleaning up after the party. Corey and her mother had been waiting in the stable block until everyone had gone.

Suddenly a pair of headlights shone in the drive.

Corey blinked. Who could *that* be? she wondered.

As the car drew closer, Corey saw that it was a horsebox. It's Jack, she realized, coming to pick up Sarah and Midnight.

The lorry stopped in front of the

stables. Corey got ready to explain what had happened.

Jack rolled down the window. "You'll never believe who I found riding along Franklin Avenue," he shouted.

Corey gasped. Sitting beside Jack in the cab of the horsebox was Mr Grover. Next to him was Sarah.

Jack jumped out of the lorry and went around to open the door for his two passengers. They dashed inside the dry stable block.

"Thank goodness you're back," Doc Tock said, hugging Sarah. "I'm not going to lecture you, Sarah, but that was a pretty foolish thing you did tonight."

"I know." Sarah blushed. "Mr Grover already told me that."

May and Jasmine came running out of the house when they saw the headlights. May hugged her father.

"Where are the horses?" Jasmine asked. "And the cart?"

"The horses are in there." Jack

pointed to the horsebox. "But we had to leave the cart by the side of the road. We'll get it tomorrow."

"You guys should have seen Hank run," Sarah said, smiling. "He might be old – but he sure can run fast!"

Mr Grover chuckled. "I'm starting to think I retired Hank too early. He managed to run all the way to the woods, then find his way to Franklin Avenue. He hasn't been that far for about five years."

"You must be a great rider, Sarah," Jasmine said. "You rode all that way in the pouring rain!"

"It was a pretty crazy ride," Sarah admitted. "I was really holding on to Midnight's mane."

"How did you find Sarah and Hank, Dad?" asked May.

"I just followed the prints in the mud," Mr Grover answered. "Once I found Sarah, we got lucky and bumped into Jack on his way to pick up her and Midnight."

Doc Tock held up a hand. "That's enough questions for now, everybody. Sarah and Mr Grover need a hot drink and dry clothes."

"I'm not going to argue with that," Mr Grover said. "But my first order of business is to get Hank home. The storm still has him pretty spooky."

"Hank's normally such a calm horse," May told the other girls. "He spooks during thunderstorms."

Jack and Mr Grover began to unload Hank and Dobbin, May's words echoed in Corey's mind.

He spooks during thunderstorms.

Slowly Corey turned to May. "Do you mean that Hank *always* acts like this?"

May nodded. "Well, he doesn't always bolt," she said. "But he always acts up. He hates storms."

"What?" Sarah piped up. "You mean the *storm* spooked Hank? Not Midnight?"

"Of course it was the storm!" May exclaimed. She grinned as she looked from Sarah to Corey. "Is that what you two thought? That Midnight did it?"

Corey blushed.

"Midnight was the one who *rescued* Hank," Jasmine pointed out. "That should prove once and for all that she's not bad luck."

The words sank in. Corey felt herself relax. Of course it had been the storm – and not Midnight – that had spooked Hank. Corey was supposed to be the most sensible member of the Pony Tails, but lately she'd been acting like the silliest one!

"Actually, one other thing proves that Midnight's not bad luck," May said, her eyes twinkling.

The three girls looked at her.

"Don't you know what today is, Sarah?" May asked.

"October twenty-ninth . . ." Sarah began. "Oh my gosh!" She clapped a

112

hand over her mouth. "I'd totally forgotten about that!"

"About what?" asked Corey.

"It's an odd day," Sarah explained. "I rode Midnight on an odd day, and nothing unlucky happened."

"Actually, something really *lucky* happened," May said. "You rescued Hank."

Just then Mr Grover led Hank down the ramp. "Hey!" he shouted. "Who put this thing on my horse?" He reached over to pull something off Hank's neck. Then he held it up for the girls to see.

May squinted to get a better look through the driving rain. "Is that a garlic necklace?" She looked at Corey and Sarah. "Did you two put that on Hank?"

But Corey and Sarah were giggling too hard to answer her question.

13
TRICK OR TREAT

"Thanks for the treats, Mrs Beyer," Jasmine said.

"You're welcome, girls," the older woman replied. "I've never had trick-or-treaters come on horseback before!"

"*Pony*back," May corrected her. "Horses are—"

But Mrs Beyer wasn't interested in hearing about the differences between horses and ponies. "Wait till I tell Mr Beyer about this," she went on. "He'll be so sorry he missed you."

The Pony Tails thanked their neighbour again. Then they turned their ponies around. The three of them, along with Sarah, had been trick-or-treating all afternoon. Luckily, they'd been able to talk Jack into driving Sarah and Midnight back over to Corey's so that she could come with them.

"I can't believe I'm riding Midnight on the thirty-first of October!" Sarah exclaimed. "Another odd day!"

Jasmine smiled. "It's a shame your pumpkin costume got ruined in the rain," she said. "But your new costume looks great, too."

Jasmine's mum had quickly put together another cowboy costume for Sarah. Now the four girls were dressed almost exactly alike. Corey gazed at her friends mounted on their

116

ponies in their Western outfits. She couldn't help smiling. Together they looked like a scene from the Wild West.

"I think we have time to stop at one more house," Jasmine said. "How about the Beekmans?"

The others quickly agreed. As Corey and Sam fell in line behind Sarah and Midnight, Sam suddenly lunged at Sarah's pony.

Before Corey could tighten the reins, he managed to nip the other pony on the tail.

"No, Sam!" Corey said sharply. "That's not nice!"

May grinned. "Sam's still not happy about having Midnight around, is he?"

"No," Corey said emphatically. "He's so rude to her!"

"Your mum says he's just being territorial," Sarah added.

"Territorial?" Jasmine repeated. "What does that mean?"

"It means Sam doesn't like sharing his space with Midnight," Corey explained. "My mother also told me that Sam's rude behaviour has helped her work out something – why she's been rude to the new vet at CARL. She doesn't like sharing her space, either."

The Pony Tails and Sarah laughed.

"Sometimes animals are a lot like people," May said.

"Well, I don't care if Sam is rude to Midnight," Sarah told Corey. "I'm just glad I don't have to worry any more about Midnight's being bad luck. How could I have believed all that stuff Mrs Lily told me?"

"I don't believe in superstitions any more, either," Corey agreed. "Except for one, that is," she added.

Jasmine looked surprised. "Which one?"

"The good-luck horseshoe at Pine Hollow," Corey said, patting Sam.

"So far it's brought me great luck. I'm going to keep rubbing it for ever."

"Makes sense to me," May said. "Just like Mrs Reg told you, some superstitions are harmless."

"Wow!" Jasmine pointed to something ahead of them. "Look at that!"

In the distance the huge autumn sun was setting. The girls stopped their ponies to watch.

As the sun sank over the tree-tops, streaks of gold and pink washed over the sky.

"It's beautiful," Corey declared.

A minute later May reminded them that it was getting late.

"Come on, pardners," she said in her best cowboy drawl. "We've got to make it back to the corral before grub time."

"Grub time?" Sarah repeated. "What's that?"

"Cowboy talk for dinnertime," Corey explained with a giggle.

119

One by one the riders gave their ponies the signal to trot across the field. Then together the four cowboys rode off into the sunset.

THE END

COREY'S TIPS ON TACKING UP YOUR PONY

Mum always tells me that taking care of a pet is a way of learning responsibility. When it comes to taking care of Sam, there's nothing I wouldn't do. The best part of owning Sam is riding him, and every time I ride him, I have to tack him up.

Before I begin tacking him up, I have to make sure he can't get loose. I tie him up using a quick-release knot then, after I've groomed him and cleaned out his hooves, he's ready to get into his riding clothes: his saddle and bridle.

First comes the saddle and numnah. A numnah is a pad that protects his back from the saddle. I put them on by setting them straight down on his withers and then sliding them along his back and into place. That does two things. Firstly, it smooths his fur down, and secondly, it gives me a chance to make sure the numnah is smooth under the saddle. If it's rumpled or lumpy, it will be very uncomfortable.

Once the saddle is in place, I check both sides of my pony to make sure the numnah is still smooth and that the saddle is properly centred. When I know everything's OK, then I'm ready to do up his girth. I make sure it's not tangled and I tighten it gently – but not as tight as I know it will be. That'll come later.

The next step is the bridle. But before I put Sam's bridle on, I unbuckle his head-collar and rebuckle it around his neck. It's a way of reminding him that there's still something holding him. Then I put the reins over his head and neck. I stand on his left side with my right shoulder next to his head. I hold the top of the bridle in my right hand and the bit in my left. Then I quietly raise the bridle over his face. As quickly and smoothly as I can, I slip the bit into his mouth. The bit's got to go over his teeth and if he won't open his mouth I tuck my thumb into the corner of his mouth, behind his teeth. I *never* knock the bit against his teeth to make him open his mouth. Before he knows it, the bit is in his mouth, behind his front teeth. Sam's good about taking the bit because I always put it in gently. And on cold days I warm the bit between my hands before I ask him to take it. I'd never hurt Sam for anything.

Once the bit is in, I slide the head-piece over his ears, being very careful not to catch his eyes. I make sure the browband is straight and that his forelock and mane are smooth, then I start to do up the buckles. I start at the ears and work down. When I do up the throat-lash, I always check too that I have the full width of my hand between it and the side of Sam's jaw bone. If it was too tight, it could inter-fere with his breathing. And when I do up the noseband, I allow two fingers' width between it and the front of his face, so that Sam can still open his mouth a bit when he needs to.

As soon as the buckles are all done up, the bridle is on. Then I unclip the lead rein and remove his head-collar.

Finally, before I can get on, I go back to the saddle and tighten the girth more. This is the part where Sam sometimes gets fussy because he doesn't like the way the girth squeezes. The thing about tightening the girth is that some ponies and horses try to fool you. They take a huge breath of air and then, once the girth is tightened, they let out the air and the girth is suddenly too loose. Sam fooled me like that once. I thought the saddle was secure and put my foot into the stirrup to mount. The whole saddle slid around until it was hanging upside down on his belly and I was flat on my back on the ground!

I said he fooled me like that *once*. He'll never do it again! Now I wait until I see him breathe out and that's when I tighten the girth. Sometimes he gives me a dirty look, but I don't mind. I know he loves me as much as I love him. More importantly, I know that he may fuss a bit when I tighten the girth, but it doesn't hurt him and in the end, we're both a lot more comfortable when the saddle is secure. (I will also check the girth again when I've been riding for ten to fifteen minutes.) When the girth is tight, I lower the stirrups and lead Sam to the paddock.

That's when he knows that we're ready for the best part. We're ready to ride.

Corey's tips checked by
Jane Harding, BHSAI

About the Author

Bonnie Bryant was born and raised in New York City, and she still lives there today. She spends her summers in a house on a lake in Massachusetts.

Ms Bryant began writing about girls and horses when she started *The Saddle Club* in 1987. So far there are more than sixty books in that series. Much as she likes telling the stories about Stevie, Carole, and Lisa, she decided that the younger riders at Pine Hollow Stables, especially May Grover, have stories of their own. That's how Pony Tails was born.

Ms Bryant rides horses when she has time away from her computer, but she doesn't have a horse of her own. She likes to ride different horses, enjoying a variety of riding experiences. She thinks most of her readers are much better riders than she is!

All Transworld titles are available by post from:

Book Service By Post, PO Box 29, Douglas, Isle of Man, IM99 1BQ

Credit cards accepted. Please telephone 01624 675137,
fax 01624 670923, Internet http://www.bookpost.co.uk
or e-mail: bookshop@enterprise.net for details

Free postage and packing in the UK. Overseas customers: allow £1 per
book (paperbacks) and £3 per book (hardbacks).